Published in the United States by Random House Children's Books,
a division of Random House, Inc., New York.

Random House and the colophon are registered trademarks
of Random House, Inc.

Visit us on the Web!
randomhouse.com/kids

Educators and librarians, for a variety of teaching tools, visit us at
randomhouse.com/teachers

Library of Congress Cataloging-in-Publication Data
Aronson, Billy.
The chicken problem / by Billy Aronson and Jennifer Oxley.
p. cm.
Summary: When someone leaves the chicken coop open
and 100 chickens escape, Peg and Cat use their math skills
to solve the problem.
ISBN 978-0-375-86989-1 (trade) — ISBN 978-0-375-96989-8 (lib. bdg.)
[1. Problem solving—Fiction. 2. Counting—Fiction. 3. Chickens—Fiction.
4. Farm life—Fiction.] I. Oxley, Jennifer, ill. II. Title.
PZ7.A7428Ch 2012 [E]—dc23 2011031249

MANUFACTURED IN CHINA   10 9 8 7 6 5 4 3 2 1   First Edition

The Chicken Problem

Jennifer Oxley + Billy Aronson

JE OXLEY
(COUNTING)

Random House 🏠 New York

This is Peg.
She loves solving problems.
She also loves pie.

This is Cat.
He loves helping Peg solve problems.
He loves pie too.

1+1=2

One day, Peg and Cat were on a farm,
getting all ready to have a perfect picnic
with a pig.

The sun was shining. The chickens were cheeping.
The pie was fresh and juicy and gooey. And
everybody had a piece of pie that was just the
right size for them. So they were ready to start
their perfect picnic with a pig, right?

2 + 1 = 3

Wrong! Peg noticed that there was
an extra piece of pie.

"BIG PROBLEM!" said Peg.

Peg felt sorry for that poor little
piece of pie, just sitting there,
all alone, with nobody to eat it!

"NOOOOOBODY!"

$3 + 1 = 4$

When Cat saw how sad Peg was, he went to
the chicken coop . . . and got a really little
chicken, to eat that really little piece of pie!
So every piece of pie had somebody!

"PROBLEM SOLVED!" said Peg,
giving Cat a great big squishy hug.

4 + 1 = 5

Now they were all ready to start
their perfect picnic with a pig.
The sun was shining.
The pie was fresh and juicy and gooey.
Everybody had a piece of pie that
was just the right size for them.
And every piece of pie had somebody.

$5 + 1 = 6$

But Peg had a feeling that
something still wasn't quite right.

What could the problem be this time?
It wasn't the sun. It wasn't the pie.
It was . . .

There were one hundred chickens going crazy
all over the place! Chickens leaping! Chickens
skipping! Chickens hopping! Chickens doing
somersaults! Chickens standing on their heads!
Chickens standing on each other's heads! Chickens
doing the chicken dance! Chickens bending
over and wiggling their bottoms in the air!
There were chickens chickens chickens chickens
chickens everywhere!

8 + 1 = q

Cat had left the door of the chicken coop open!
So the farmer's one hundred chickens
had gotten out of the coop!

"REALLY BIG PROBLEM!" said Peg.

Peg and Cat and the pig got right to work
picking up the chickens. As they picked up
chickens, Cat danced a little dance and Peg
sang a little song:

"PICKIN' UP CHICKENS!
ONE CHICK-EE!"

"CALLIN' ALL CHICKENS!
COME TO ME!"

9+1=10

"PEEKABOO, CHICKEN!
COME OUT OF THAT SHOE!"

"PICKIN' UP CHICKENS!
NOW I'VE GOT TWO!"

"PICKIN' UP CHICKENS!
ONE TWO THREE!"

"I'VE GOT CHICKENS
ALL OVER ME!"

10+1=11

"NOW TAKE YOUR CHICKENS
TO THE COOP AND BE QUICK!
A-CHICKA CHICKA CHICKA CHICKA
CHICKA CHICK CHICK!"

When they reached the coop,
Peg couldn't believe how many chickens
they had carried.

1 2 3 4 5 6 7 8 9

11+1=12

"THAT'S ONE, TWO, THREE, FOUR, FIVE, SIX, SEVEN, EIGHT, NINE, TEN CHICKENS BACK IN THE COOP!"

said Peg.

So the problem was solved.
Right?

12+1=13

Wrong!

There were still so many chickens left! Chickens dashing! Chickens splashing! Chickens skipping! Chickens flipping! Chickens swinging! Chickens singing! Chickens bouncing! Chickens pouncing! Chickens sliding! Chickens riding! Chickens spinning around and around! Chickens rolling all over the ground! Chickens hanging upside down! There were more chickens than Peg could count using all her fingers! And all her toes! And all of Cat's fingers and toes too!

Peg begged the chickens
to go back to the coop.
She tried chasing them.

She tried racing them.

She tried jumping up and down
and commanding the chickens
to go back to the coop.
But nothing worked!

15+1=16

"I'LL NEVER GET THOSE ONE HUNDRED CHICKENS BACK IN THE COOP!"

"THEY'LL KEEP RUNNING WILD AND GOING CRAZY ALL OVER THE PLACE FOREVER AND EVER AND EVER AND EVER AND EVER AND

I AM TOTALLY FREAKING OUT!"

16 + 1 = 17

When Cat saw Peg freaking out,
he held up his hands
to get her to calm down.

So Peg took a deep breath and counted:

"FIVE ... FOUR ... THREE ...
TWO ... ONE ..."

17 + 1 = 18

And as she counted, Peg noticed that Cat's tail
seemed to be pointing to a pile of wheely things:
two wheelbarrows and a baby carriage.
"YES! THAT'S A GREAT IDEA,
YOU AMAAAAAZING CAT!"

18 + 1 = 19

Peg separated the wheely things
and put them in a row.

"HEY, CHICKENS! WHO WANTS TO
GO FOR A RIDE?"

In a flash, the chickens dashed
into the wheely things!
(Chickens really love going for a ride.)

19+1=20

Peg, the pig, and Cat each got behind
the wheely thing that was
just the right size for them.

"ONE, TWO, THREE, PUSH!"

said Peg, and they started to push.

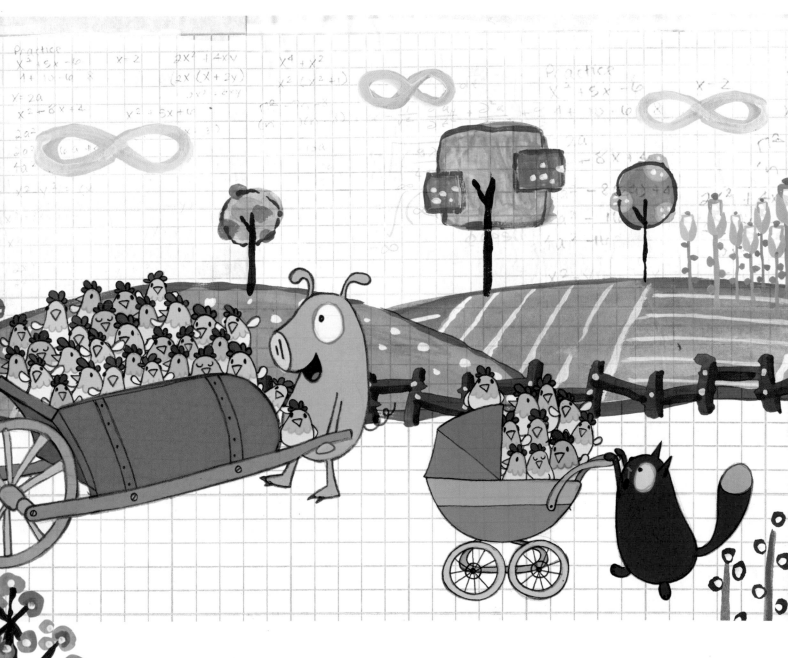

"HOLD ON TIGHT, LITTLE CHICKIE-CHICKS.
YOU'RE GOIN' HOME!"

20+1=21

When all the chickens (except for the really
little chicken) were safe and snug in their coop,
Cat closed the door.

"PROBLEM SOLVED!"
said Peg, giving Cat
a great big squishy hug.

21+1=22

Then Peg, Cat, and the pig went
back to the picnic blanket,
and Cat set the little chicken
down beside him.

The sun was shining.
The chickens were sleeping.
The pie was fresh and juicy and gooey.
Everybody had a piece of pie that was
just the right size for them.
And every piece of pie had somebody.
So they were finally ready to have
their perfect picnic with a pig. Right?

22 + 1 = 23

23+1=24

"RIGHT!"

24 + 1 = 25

The authors would like to give special thanks to:

Kate Klimo, Cathy Goldsmith, Chip Gibson, and Rich Romano
at Random House for publishing the book!

Dennis Kostyk for making the connection!

Julie Kane-Ritsch and Jonathan Herzog
for doing the contracts!

Linda Simensky and Kim Berglund at PBS
for doing everything they do!

And, for posing so patiently for the pictures,
the one hundred chickens:
Fluffy, Little Yellow, Benny Beak, Claws, Ol' Tail Feathers,
Puffy, Clucky, Triple Cheep McGee, Polly Peck, Egg Man,
Chick Corea, Screech, Awk, Bakaww, Barawk Obama,
Michele Squawkmann, Lady Cawcaw, Imogen Cheep, Mellow Yellow,
Curious Yellow, Chick It Out, Chick Your Bags, Chick Please,
Here A. Chick, There A. Chick, Everywhere A. Chick-Chick,
Cluck "Cheeps" Martin, Cheep "Clucks" Bottini,
Cluck Cluck Cheep Cheep Martin-Bottini,
Cockadoodledoo Horowitz, Cluck C. Cluck III, Seedy Sue,
Chicken Little, Chicken Big, Chicken Size Doesn't Matter,
Wyatt Chirp, St. John the Chicken, Wolfgang Amadeus Chicken,
George Bernard Chicken, Charles Chickens,
Her Royal Highness Mary Queen of Chickens, Mahatma Chicken,
Mao Tse Chicken, Charlie "Bird" Chicken,
The Artist Formerly Known as Chicken,
Little Red Riding Chicken, Rumpelchicken,
Chip, Chirp, Chap, and all fifty members
of the South Carolina Marching Band of Chickens!